Fantastical Tales for the Heroine's Quest

Annie Razz

PublishAmerica
Baltimore

First printing

ISBN: 1-4241-0424-6
PUBLISHED BY PUBLISHAMERICA, LLLP
www.publishamerica.com
Baltimore

Printed in the United States of America

In memory and honor of
Cecelia Beuligmann
1936-2005
5th grade teacher

Acknowledgments

I wish to thank everyone who has supported me in this most recent quest—the publication of this book. This includes all my family and friends. I would like to especially thank Jim Cooley, Curtis Urness, Sr. and Cheryl Chavez for their excellent editing advice. Special recognition goes to Marci and Jem Rasmussen for the patience and love they have shown which has made this book possible.

I would also like to note the unflagging enthusiasm of Marcella Inman, Gordon Inman, Douglas Inman, Marsha Miller, Kathleen Winn, Ellen Quinly, Andie Swan and my co-workers at Wyandot Center, Kansas City, Kansas. A special recognition goes to all my clients, especially the children who inspire me every day. There are also those people from long ago who always believed in my writing—Lani Hudson, Mary Murguia, Diane DeArmond and Samuel Zentner.

This book would not be possible without the influence of the Westport Writer's Group, the Institute of Children's Literature and the Greater Kansas City Writing Project.

Lastly, I thank PublishAmerica for publishing America and giving voice to so many whose voices enhance our lives.

Fantastical Tales for the Heroine's Quest

Every girl is on a quest. Every woman lives a life of fantastic tales. Every female is a heroine. To be female in America is to travel a road that was not paved for you. Travel it you do, though, either as a wild adventure or a carefully planned trip. Along the way you discover your power, talents and strengths as you become your true, best self.

The trip is exciting, but not without peril. You may find dragons and witches in the guise of cruel peers, uncaring authority or hapless companions. You might find yourself fighting for your right to even be on the road. Then again, you may dance along singing in glorious celebration of this marvelous adventure called life.

It is hard, yet wonderful, to be a girl in the modern world. *What is the truth? Who do I believe? What is best for me?* Every female must look to *her* own heart and use *her* own best sense as the compass that will navigate her safely through the feminine journey to her best self. It is a quest that never really ends, though there are many breathtaking stops along the way. The stories and poems in *Fantastical Tales for the Heroine's Quest* speak to the wonder of this journey. These stories of friendship, love, fear and victory offer the magic of faith and belief that can help guide you in your own personal quest.

When we live our lives as an adventure, we create stories that illustrate who we are. Our stories help us understand why we do what we do. *Fantastical Tales for the Heroine's Quest* are stories that illuminate the feminine archetype. These are tales of the maiden's transformation into what every girl always becomes — a bigger, better version of herself — a woman!

Fantastical Tales for the Heroine's Quest is a collection of stories and poems for the young woman, the teenage girl, or anyone with an open heart who yearns to live her truest truth. These tales are written for that soulful heart that will always beat loud. They are written for the female spirit that is bravely and beautifully meeting each day with the courage and audacity of a warrioress. They are written for the modern girl, no matter her age, who still hears a song in her heart, believing good will prevail.

They are written for *you*.

Table of Contents

Chapter One

If My Life Were a Myth

I am an eternal girl.
I am walking through the day as if it were maybe going to be
magic
just this once…
signs tumble from the heavens—
in slow motion truth they shimmer in the sun
then fall into the shade
so that I ask, "What did I see, or did I?"
The ground is a magnet which will not let me fly. My eyes
watch in disbelief at the scenes that unfold,
leading me to places
I never knew I wanted to be.
I ask for guidance, wondering why I hear nothing but the
fluttering of my own heart.
Mostly life is boring.
Mostly life is full.

Chapter Two

Three Sisters

Deep in the Babushka woods, the woods of the grandmother, three sisters often visited. They were Yeska, Maybeka and Noka. Actually, they weren't sisters at all, but just girls who knew and loved one another in that nonchalant way that sisters have.

Yeska was the oldest of the three, which she mentioned often, as if it gave her the right to lead, but it was really only the mentioning of it all the time that made the other two roll their eyes and say, "Okay, Yeska, we'll do what you want AGAIN." Then they did, for a little while, but usually, after a bit, Maybeka would have engineered them quietly in a whole other direction where they all went without noticing anything was askew. Sometimes Noka would lead them entirely in another direction herself. They usually did notice this since it often involved falling off cliffs or climbing trees that had bark which made little steps going up, but set itself more like little daggers going down.

This Tuesday, Yeska was leading them again to the edge of the great divide. The great divide was not really all that great nor even a true divide. It was a river that ran through the darkest part of the woods if they followed it long enough.

"I don't want to go," Noka said. "I don't want to follow that path because I don't like the darkness it goes through, and anyway, we know where it leads."

"But once we get through the darkness, and surely we will this time, we'll get to the place where the gems lay. You know that. It'll pay for my tuition into the best school money can buy," Yeska seemed to almost whine.

Noka looked at Maybeka for help. For some reason Yeska listened to Maybeka a little more than to her.

But Maybeka only answered, "Noka, let's go. For just a bit. It will be an adventure. And you do like adventures. I know you do!"

It was true. Noka did like adventures, but Yeska usually led them on what felt more like an ordeal. There was a difference.

Yeska did not wait for the other two. Everyone knew she was right. That was her way. The right way.

"The river is here. It calls to us." Yeska laughed, making her voice sound like a gurgling brook.

Or more like a babbling one, Noka thought.

Maybeka moved closer to Yeska, but it was toward Noka that she looked imploringly.

"It is a beautiful river," she said. "See how it shines promising blue like the sky?"

"That's not the point," Noka said. "It is pretty. It may be promising, but it isn't promising anything I want."

Noka looked up at the mountaintops peeking out above the tips of the trees.

"What's wrong with you? Why don't you want gems?" Yeska said in a way that sounded more like an accusation than a question.

"Gems are great," Noka said. "But the gems at the end of the river, well, they are the same gems everyone has. We aren't even sure the river leads to gems. That is just what 'They' say. Besides, I think there might be some other gems elsewhere that shine differently."

Noka's eyes shined differently when she said this. Maybeka had noticed this before when Noka looked at the mountains while they were on the river path, or when she looked at the silvery currents of the river as they were bouncing and bounding through the ocean. Sometimes the shine seemed a little scary, a little too bright, unlike the shininess of the stars and the moon that Maybeka so adored.

"I know," Maybeka called out suddenly. "Let's follow the river, but follow it upstream this time toward the mountains."

Yeska's face blanched. "Up the river? No one does that anymore. It is so passé. That is like going backwards. I would know, having been around a little longer than you two."

"Forget the river altogether. I am going my own way!" Noka said, grabbing her knapsack, slinging it over her shoulder and running into the trees.

"She will catch up later," Yeska said. "She is a smart girl and will come to her senses."

"Hmm," Maybeka said, as if that were an answer.

She and Yeska made their way down the river. Now and then Maybeka glanced around for Noka, but Yeska was right. Noka was a big girl and could make her own decisions. Going down river to the gems was a profitable adventure, even though it did mean those dark days where no light could make it through the trees and going through the swampland of venomous vipers and the gluey ponds of shrimp with teeth. She looked at Yeska, whose eyes seemed to gleam, too. Maybeka wondered if it was because of the challenge or something else. She wondered if her own eyes shined.

Meanwhile, Noka tramped to the edge of the woods, swinging her knapsack as if it was the magic blade of a medieval swashbuckler slashing through all the vines and tendrils and what were possibly girl-eating snakes that hurled their long slithery bodies into her path.

As she whacked her way through, she stumbled once or twice on the gnarled roots that seemed to leap out of the ground. Not only that, but little opossum pits kept catching her toes and made her fall forward in a most unbecoming way.

Still she foraged ahead, even as she became more and more tired. It was only midmorning, but she felt she could not go an inch further. She curled up in the leafy debris, making a bed as best as she could. The leaves smelled dank and muddy and maybe a little of rot. She inhaled deeply.

"Ah, the smell of freedom," she said as her thoughts meandered quietly into sleep.

She didn't notice the nightshade plants sneaking up, weaving their tendrils about her feet. She didn't notice the brown recluse spiders coming out for a peek. She didn't notice the covey of rare bloodsucking owls swooping incongruously onto the unsteady branches swaying above her head. Perhaps it is because she didn't notice them that they did not harm her, for she slept peacefully and soundly.

She woke to the sun shining at its full-noon highest. She dug into her knapsack to see what food she might find. *Drat*. She thought she had packed some nuts for their high unsaturated fat content and heavy duty protein boost, but there were none. There were a couple of squirrels snickering about two or three yards away. Hmm. Why was it in fairytales the little animals always helped the fair maiden and in her life the squirrels were, well, squirrels?

She stretched and got up, picking the nettles from her hair. She tromped around until she found a couple of walnuts that she placed on a rock. She chose another rock and smashed down hard. She could've sworn she saw a squirrel taking notes, but then that was not possible since her life wasn't a fairytale after all. It was not even a corporately funded major Hollywood studio animated movie. However, it was magic in its own way because the rock she chose to be the smasher broke almost evenly down the middle to expose an inside of glittery columns and jagged chips of crystal. How beautiful it was. She sat it back down on the forest floor. Not as a gift to the squirrels, because they didn't deserve anything, she thought, but more as…what? A talisman, yes. The rock would serve as a talisman to remind the world of its wonder, in case the world ever forgot. She crunched the walnuts, picked a few mint leaves and on she went.

The river rose to her right; its waters gleaming silver in the sun. *It does make sense to follow the river for the fresh water and fish,* she thought, but then she looked over the meadow covered with golden rod, milkweed and buttercups. Fingers of the meadow slipped into the crevices of the craggy mountainside. Noka sighed. As if she were some girl from Kansas walking into a poppy field, she slid into the landscape, her head held high. She sang out, her voice also rising high into a lilt as if she were in some old-fashioned musical. This is when Noka realized she watched far too many movies. She wondered if this was where she got the notion that following her own path would work out in the end. But now she knew there were no scripts or best boys or film archival specialists to influence her way. She walked as well as she could through the field, trying not to break the necks of the innocent flowers. She had the uncanny feeling that some unseen movie director might call out "cut!" any minute. It was not a particularly pleasant feeling.

She placed her hand to her forehead in an ultra-dramatic way, saying, "Ah, the heat, the hope, the impossibility of a life lived only true to itself…" No doubt she had much more to say, but she was rudely interrupted by what sounded like a billy goat gruff.

"What the…" she said, spinning around. It was not a billy goat—or at least not the sort that walked on four legs. It was the sort that walked on two legs. He looked like he might butt into something at any moment.

"Just who are you," she asked, "ruining my opera-like diva moment the way you just did?"

"Oh, is that what it was? I thought it was the pollen getting to you."

"You seem to be the one snorting," Noka said. "At least I am going somewhere and it is obvious that you are not, even though you seem to have three legs."

She looked at the boy closer, suddenly realizing what she thought was his third leg was really a walking stick.

"Hey," he said, covering up parts of himself that she had not even been looking at.

Noka blushed. This would not do. Blushing always seemed to accompany her going somewhere she did not particularly want to go. Thinking quickly, she held out her left hand. "Nice to meet you. I am Noka."

He only laughed again. "No what?" he asked.

"What?" she asked back, as if he had said "know" and not "no."

"What?" he answered back himself, but "what" is not so much an answer as another question and sadly enough this may have gone on for hours if it had not been for the great purple winged creature that glided above their heads, making them both look up almost straight into the sun.

"Yikes," Noka said when she shaded her eyes enough to see the great flapping Thing circling around, its path veering in a downward direction toward them.

"Run," the boy shouted.

Noka did not like to take direction from anyone and certainly not someone she had just met, and even more certainly not from a boy, but running did seem a good idea. She didn't quibble with the suggestion. She instead ran as fast as she could. They both raced toward a cave at the base of the mountain where a pinkie fingerlet of the meadow seemed to point.

Noka slid into the cave like it was first base, but the boy slid as if it was home plate. He landed smack dab on top of her like a swoop bike crashing.

"Call me, Hans," he said.

Noka had no intention of calling him anything.

Maybeka followed Yeska sullenly, hopping half-heartedly over the muddy rivulets that scored the river's banks. *My new hip hop mock croc boots might get ruined*, she thought absent-mindedly, when she noticed a purple plant with a whitish underneath.

"Look, a purple waffle plant," she said, jumping back as if the waffle plant had sprung from a toaster.

"Yum," Yeska said, reaching for the plant. "I'm starving."

"Ooh, don't. It's poisonous. At least to cats."

"Ah," Yeska said, bowing her head, "That's right, Fluffy."

Maybeka wiped a tear from her eye. "That doesn't make me a murderer, you know?"

"Oh, of course not," Yeska said. "Wasn't it sold as a sister plant to the fruit salad plant at Terrarium Delirium? I would blame it entirely on them, though how they would have known you were buying it as an accompaniment to your catnip garden only God knows."

"Don't bring God into this," Maybeka said. "You know I am an optimistic agnostic and before you know it you will be going on and on about Fluffy's soul, which feels like proselytizing to me."

"Hey," Yeska said," I think someone is a little testy from lack of food."

"Me?" asked Maybeka. "I just finished those hickory nuts and chickpeas we found a ways back."

"So?" Yeska said, her eyes filling with tears. "I would give anything for some bread fruit and maybe some jelly fruit to go with it."

Maybeka looked up quickly, only to see Yeska's big smile. They both laughed, but only for a moment. Maybeka felt guilty laughing without Noka.

"Do you think we should go look for Noka?" she asked.

"No," Yeska said. "We know where she is. Basically, she's wasting her time on a fruitless journey."

She smiled again, but Maybeka did not laugh.

"Whatever. I might as well go with you for awhile," Maybeka said, "After all, there are a lot of exotic plants and animals on this stretch of the river. You know how happy they make me. A moment of joy in this Godless world unless, of course, God is real, then it is not a Godless world, but still maybe joyless. Although I'm not all that unhappy, you see the point I am trying to make is…is…"

"The point is that you have no point," Yeska said. "And you will miss out if you don't follow me. You will be sorry, but I will tell you all about it. Noka, too and you will both say, 'If only, if only' and I will say, 'It could've been you holding mountains of gems' and everyone else will say, 'You should have, you should have.'"

Maybeka looked at Yeska as if Yeska's bushy beetle eyebrows had sprouted wings. They had not. In fact, the only wings within miles were those beating furiously as a speeding some Thing raced toward them. The very air reverberated. Each girl heard the other scream. Both closed their eyes and prayed. Even Maybeka.

Noka and Hans scuttled as deep into the cave as they could and still keep the arc of sunlight ringing the entrance within their sight. Noka pulled back from the cave wall where green tinted water trickled down.

"What?" Hans said as she bumped against him in her haste to get away from the wall.

"I don't like moss juice," she said.

"Moss juice?" Hans asked.

"You sure seem to ask a lot of questions, but not so much give answers." Noka said grumpily, because that was her way.

"Okay. Here's an answer for you: There is no such thing as moss juice."

Noka raised her eyebrows, not in surprise, but in shock.

"There is," she said with a Yeska sort of certainty. She liked how it felt as if she were a new and improved version of herself. She looked closer at the moss juice.

"Uh, oh," she said, realizing it was water indeed.

She thought then perhaps it would have been better off sounding like her old self because now Hans was right. This was not a problem in itself, but it, by default made her wrong. She thought of how her sisters would tease her when she was wrong until she would blush and scoot away to hide from them until they could be nice again.

But before she could apologize or anything, Hans said, "Uhm, well, uhm, I guess this mountain is full of some things I didn't know about, like moss juice and..."

"Purple Things with wings!" Noka finished for him as a witch with spaghetti-like hair and an enormous dark lavender cape filled the entrance of the cave. The witch's face was covered with warts that stuck out like eyes on a potato. Everything grew dark.

"Stand back, Maybeka," Yeska shouted wildly, scouring the ground for a weapon of some sort. But there was not one nor could she figure out fast enough what to make into one. The Thing swooped down. It grabbed Maybeka with its great claws, and then dashed fast back into the sky.

Yeska shouted even louder, but of course a shout does not a weapon make. The Thing flew away with her sister in its clutches.

Yeska fell to the ground, weeping what seemed to be gallons of tears as she pulled at her hair.

"No, no, no!" she cried.

After a few minutes when crying and pulling did not bring her sister back Yeska pulled herself up. She wiped the teary mud from her face and looked into the sky empty of purple Things. It was also empty of sisters. All she saw was the sun was moving closer to the horizon.

She knew soon it would be time to eat. Maybe the purple Thing did not want to eat Maybeka, but maybe it did. Yeska may have had choices. She could have sat down and made a fire for her own dinner and wished her sister luck. She could have fallen back down in a weeping fit, but she was not aware of these choices. She was only aware of impending doom, and though she might be no match for the flying evil that kidnaped her sister, she would be the most she could. She began walking as a soldier into war. She did not stop as the sun moved further down the sky. She did not stop as hunger pangs growled, then gnawed, at her empty stomach because her empty heart was all she noticed as she tromped ever forward.

It was almost dusk when she noticed Noka's knapsack in the brambles next to a path leading into a crevice. Yeska looked around as if she were just waking. Why, she was now in the mountains. She had not even noticed the gradual incline, but now felt her calves stinging, or was it her heart as she realized that if Noka left her knapsack behind it meant she had either given up all her worldly possessions to live a life of free abandon, or that she too, was waylaid on her journey. Yeska did not think she could bear losing two sisters, her two best friends. But she knew she would have to bear whatever she would have to bear. That is the way of reality. It does not always give you what you ask or ask you back how you would like it to be. Reality had its own way that it did no good to fight against. No matter how you try, you can't really boss around reality as much as it bosses you around, Yeska realized.

"I will float, I will flow. I will bear it well," she said aloud.

"Bear?" a voice cried, "No, not bears now!"

Yeska swung around. The voice sounded like Maybeka's, but that would have been just a little too coincidental. But then reality was not just bossy, it was also serendipitous.

Yeska felt hope growing in her middle like a warm lantern lighting her inside.

"Maybeka!" she called as loud as she could, her hands in karate position in case Maybeka was still in the claws of the Thing.

"Yes! Yes! Yes!" the voice cried.

Each yes got louder until Maybeka was right there in front of Yeska, then on top of her. Both girls hugged, screaming like wild banshees.

"Speaking of wild banshees..." Maybeka said, pulling away.

"We weren't speaking of banshees. We were sounding like them," Yeska corrected her, but then remembered to go with the flow and added, "But who cares, and what is it about your eyes? They seem brighter."

Maybeka didn't notice Yeska's bossiness because she had what she had to say and what Yeska said or did not say would not change what she had to say. But she did hear what Yeska had said about her eyes. She blinked them several times.

"It was a banshee who stole me away."

"That purple Thing?"

"The purple is a robey capey drape she wears. It is what gives her power to believe in herself more than what she does normally."

"Wow! Did she tell you this?"

"Not with words, but her actions. Her eyes will look scared, and then she will whip the robe around growing proud, which she tries to prove with rude proclamations like, 'To resist is futile' or 'My way or the highway.'"

"Man, she's not even original."

"I don't think you have to be original when you are that powerful," Maybeka said.

"At least she didn't eat you. Speaking of food..." Yeska plopped down to look to see if there might be an errant hickory nut or two at the bottom of Noka's knapsack.

"You shouldn't really be messing with Noka's knapsack, you know. Now that you mention banshees, where is Noka, and why is she not in fashionable proximity to her accessories?"

"Maybe," Yeska said, " because the reason the witch didn't eat you is that she ate Noka!"

"No! No!" Maybeka shouted. "I will not even imagine Noka's dead, or give that thought any power. Anyway, the banshee didn't eat me because she doesn't eat people. I forgot to tell you that part."

Noka didn't believe in liking boys in a like/like way, so she had never held a guy's hand, but this didn't stop her from grabbing Hans' left hand.

"I've got a plan," she said. "Let's knock her over."

"My thoughts exactly," he said.

Noka doubted that, but this hardly seemed the time for a debate. Instead, she rolled her eyes. "Are you ready?" she asked.

Hans wasn't used to holding a girl's hands himself, but he didn't drop Noka's now. They both stood up in unison.

"I am ready," he said. "I'll lead and you follow."

"It is my idea and I will lead," Noka said.

"Well, it was my idea, too. I just didn't say it," Hans said.

"Whatever," Noka said, not bothering to argue any longer as she leapt toward the witch. Hans was pulled along just a millisecond behind her. He would've argued, but he was too busy trying to keep up with her.

They flew through the air like speeding starships aiming for the witch's center of gravity.

The witch was potato-like and tall. She had muscles from all her flying. The two could not knock her down. They bounced off. The witch made a low gurgle-like noise as she slowly, yet menacingly tromped toward them. Her cape opened wide. It fluttered about her like batwings.

This gave Noka her second idea. She ran deeper into the cave, though it was very dark. It got darker the farther she went. Hans followed her, not because he trusted her or because he believed in like/like, but because she was still holding his left hand.

When they were deep, deep into the cave, Noka slid farther into a shadow. She didn't care if moss juice got on her or not.

She whispered her plan to Hans as the witch crept closer and closer. The cave had gotten narrower, the roof much lower. Both Noka and Hans were much shorter than the witch. Neither had eaten much for awhile now so they were a little bit skinnier. The witch was bent over, almost crawling so that she seemed much smaller than she had before. The cape which once had looked like wings was now damp and wilted, wet and torn.

"Now!" Noka shouted, speeding full force forward as if she was the one with wings. Hans did the same. The witch didn't have time nor room to spread her cape. The two swept past her on either side.

Neither Noka nor Hans stopped until they both were out of breath, their sides feeling like they were splitting. Noka held her stomach. Hans fell down exhausted.

"Good job!" Noka huffed.

"Ditto," Hans said.

Hans is turning out to be really a good friend or ally, and what really is the difference, Noka thought. How odd to be able to have such a great adventure with another neither making fun of you nor bossing you around. *Well, he was kind of bossy, or at least acted like he wanted to be, but nothing ever really came of his bossiness,* she thought. She liked that about him. Not only that but he was also sort of cute, even though he was a boy and boys were so strange.

"Maybe we can…" she began, but did not finish, because even though they had run very fast they forgot the witch had powers they did not.

Noka lost her breath as the witch's claws swung down again. Whoosh! She was in the air.

But Noka was not one to say yes, nor even maybe. She was one to say no. She did so now, not just with her mouth, but her body. She arched her back and twisted her left side to the right so that she was able to wring herself free. She plummeted to the ground like an apple falling from a tree.

Hans ran up to her still body. The witch did not land, but flew off into the darkening sky. Hans thought he could hear her cackling yet, for some reason, it didn't sound so much like a laugh as it did a wail of despair.

Hans put his ear to Noka's mouth. Was she breathing?

"You forgot to tell me what part?" Yeska was feeling irritable by now.

"The witch, she didn't take me to eat. She took me because she is lonely. She doesn't know how to make friends."

"Wow. I can see how she would have trouble, being so gruesome-looking and well, snatching innocent people and terrorizing them to near death can't be too helpful, either."

"She doesn't want to do that. She just feels like she has to, like she doesn't have any other choices."

"She needs to go to choice school then, because that just doesn't rock."

"Look, there she goes now!" Maybeka jumped up, flailing her arms as if she were a survivor on an island trying to get a biplane's attention. Where was the camera crew and reality TV show personnel when you needed them?

Apparently the flailing worked because the witch slowly powered down toward them.

"What!" Yeska screamed. It is one thing to make friends with a demonic wraith from the netherworlds, as Maybeka apparently had, but it is quite another to invite her for a nighttime picnic.

"Give it a rest, Yeska. I told you she's not evil."

"Oh, yeah, I forgot. She just acts evil. Well, in my world evil is as evil does."

"Oh, there you go, getting all smiley-facey. Life's not that simple. Hello, Wanda!"

Maybeka strolled over to the rumpled purple heap that had crash-landed about twenty yards over.

Wanda sat up, her face streaked with tears.

"What is it?" Maybeka asked, wiping away the tears. "Did you get hurt landing?"

"Noooooooooooooo," Wanda wailed. "It is not me I cry for, but you."

Maybeka's heart leaped in fear for a split second. Had she gotten it all wrong? Was Yeska right as usual? Was Wanda going to now kill her and eat her?

"M-m-me?" she asked.

"Yes, because of your sister. Well, you see, I, she, it was dark, uhm, well...I dropped her."

"You mean like you got to be friends with her, then you decided not to be friends and you dropped her?" Maybeka knew in her heart of hearts that was not what Wanda meant, but sometimes hope springs up in the strangest of times to keep the truth away for just another minute or so.

"No. Dropped her like smash, smack, ground, hard, hurt."

Maybeka's mouth dropped open even though she knew it was not a good look for her. Her lips trembled, but no words came out.

Yeska had no trouble finding words.

"Why, you fiend!" she said, rising up from where she had been hiding behind a bush watching the two.

She ran toward Wanda, this time with a weapon that would work, a limb from the honeysuckle bush that had broken off when Wanda crashed. She raised the limb and brought it down. THWACK! Hard on Wanda's head.

"No!" Maybeka screamed.

Hans dragged Noka's body back to the cave. He figured it would be best to keep it safe from any wolves or other meat-eating Things that might defile what was left of her. He took off

31

his jean jacket, custom screen-printed with a picture of a director's chair and a bullhorn. He placed it on top of her. He tore off the bottom cuff of his khakis to swab the blood off the back of her head. He wiped the dirt off her face with the drips of water sliding down the cave's wall. They weren't green anymore and he looked up to see a hole in the cave's roof. It must have been the sunlight glinting through the leafy foliage that had tinted the water green to look like moss juice. *Oh, back in the day,* he thought, *how nice it was then when Noka still breathed and life was good. Well, not so good because we were running away from a witch and all, but still—things are always better when you are alive,* he thought philosophically as he lay next to Noka, holding her close.

He was comforted by the warmth her dead body still provided. He drowsily began falling into sleep lulled by the quiet rhythm of…of…of her heart! Her heart! She *was* alive after all. Hans stood up and raised his hands to the starry sky he could see through the hole in the cave's roof.

"Thank you, God!" he called out.

And perhaps it was God who answered, or maybe just happenstance, but either way Noka opened her eyes slowly and called out…"I'm blind! I'm blind! I can't see!"

"No, it is only dark, my love," Hans said, kneeling to touch her face.

"Whose love? What?" Noka said, feeling more than awake now as she sat up so fast she toppled Hans over.

"Uhhhh," Hans didn't know what else to say because he had already said too much. He said nothing more but looked down.

This made Noka look down, too. It is interesting how two people sometimes match their actions almost like their movements are dancing without them knowing it. Looking down, she noticed Hans' ripped pants, his jacket curled up, wet and dirty on the cave's floor. She looked up slowly to see his face streaked with dried tears, or perhaps he had sweated really hard. Either way.

She didn't say anything back to make him feel better because she also didn't know what to say. But she did reach out her hand to touch his. His fingers folded about hers. Together they stood up.

"Shall we stay, or shall we go now?" she asked because wasn't that the most important question now…not what did he mean by "my love."

"The cave is safe," he said.

"But home is through the darkness," Noka said.

Hans nodded. She was right. Though they may have had choices, they didn't really. They walked out of the cave into the night.

They had only walked a short way before they stumbled over Maybeka and Yeska fighting in the shadows.

"You act without thinking and run into things like a chicken with no head!" Maybeka groused angrily.

"Well, that's better than being wishy-washy, looking at both sides and never taking a stand so that wraiths like wicked witches can come and eat you up." Yeska clucked.

"But I'm not even hungry, and even if I were, I'm a vegetarian," a voice coming from over by the broken honey suckle bush chirped in.

Noka looked closer and saw that it was a potatoey looking woman in a purple cape.

"Look, Hans," she said. "Is it the witch?"

"You mean two witches," he answered, looking at her sisters.

"No, not them, they are my best friends. I mean over there…in the bushes, is it the witch?"

However, he had no time to answer because she screamed, suddenly realizing she was reunited with her sisters.

"Yeska, Maybeka!" she shouted over their shouts. "I'm home."

Of course, none of them were really home, but perhaps it feels like home when you are with those you love.

"Oh, Noka!" both Maybeka and Yeska cried in unison, dropping their squabbling to rush up to their sister. They squeezed her half to death.

When they pulled apart, all three spoke in unison again, *in a very quantum physics sort of way,* Noka thought, wondering what the blazes all this synchronicity was about.

They all asked, "But who is that?" Yeska and Maybeka pointed to Hans. Noka pointed to Wanda.

Everyone introduced everyone else. Noka and Hans were very surprised to find that Wanda was not out to kill them, though she almost did kill Noka by mistake.

"I suppose it was more my fault than anything," Noka said, trying to comfort this homely woman who seemed sweeter by the moment, maybe because she was sharing honeysuckle she kept plucking from the honeysuckle bush she had knocked over.

"No, it was my fault because I scared you. You might not have tried to twist away if you hadn't been scared."

"That's true," Noka agreed. "It is your fault, but I forgive you. Do you forgive her, Hans?"

"Yes," Hans said, but he didn't say anything more because he didn't want to pressure Noka. He didn't want to make her feel weird by saying he secretly was glad it had all happened like it had because that is how it came to be that they had fallen in love or at least extra special-like.

He mostly didn't say anything more to Noka because Yeska and Maybeka were talking his head off. He was the first boy to enter their world of three. They found him quite fascinating. Maybeka wondered how he would fit, but then thought he would fit as well as Wanda would. That is how families grow, she thought, not unlike beautiful weeds in a garden.

Noka hoped there would be many more adventures ahead. Maybe future adventures could feature more food and not always end in the dark. She reached out and touched Hans as if he were a talisman. He was cute no matter what he had meant by that freaky love comment. Boys could be so strange.

"Thank you, God," Maybeka said, hurriedly adding, "If there is a God." But she knew there was as surely as fate twists and turns us down different paths so that we each end up where we never knew we wanted to be.

Yeska thought of gems and expensive schools. *Maybe education doesn't have to cost so much, but then maybe it does,* she thought, looking down at the scuffs on her designer boots.

All of them sat back after they had eaten their full of honeysuckle. They watched the stars, one by one, color the sky in hues that seemed to keep changing.

"Some days are just like magic and those are the best days of all," Hans said, reaching for Noka's left hand.

Noka smiled to herself. With her other hand she reached out for Yeska's, who in turn held Maybeka's hand. Maybeka held Wanda's. Hands entwined, they all lay back under the night sky.

"No matter how dark it gets there will be stars or a moon or friends to light the way," Wanda said. She was right.

Chapter Three

Poems of the Imagination

Fairy Wish

Oh, to be a fairy—
tiny & small,
flying about,
climbing the walls—
only to be caught
in a spider's snare
or squashed by a bottom
in an easy chair.
But think of the magic!
How fun it would be!
Flinging fairy dust—
wild and free…
sneezing & coughing…
choking to death
&
with your very last fairy breath,
you'd say that though
being a fairy was swell & keen,
you'd rather have been
a human being.

Treasure Map

My life unfolds like a treasure map, gold and green.
I don't know where it will lead me
or if I'll end up where I've already been.
A snowless mountain looms like magic.
Rain falls like tea on a starlit night.
A cave beckons slyly,
its shadows so black they shine white.
I walk to where the line crosses and makes a gorgeous X.
I scream to Heaven to help me throw love like a hex.
I get no help but from the map, now ragged and torn.
Heaven hasn't talked to me since the day I was born.
I carry the map in a furious fist,
searching for my path in the map's turns and twists.

A Fish Tale

You're a shark
& I'm your fish friend.
You're a nice shark who only eats
fish who are fiends or offend
or do something I don't do
or if I do it, I do it less
& in a way that makes you smile but not eat me.
You being a shark is great because it means you can protect
me.
You glint your teeth & mean fish swim away
as I snuggle closer, though your skin is cold
& brrr—I shake inside as you swim away
to skirt the seas for lurking dangers
I cannot see.
Once an angel fish says she saw you
at a sand bar drinking with an electric eel.
A seagull said he saw you winking at a humpbacked whale.
But I don't believe them. I believe you.
You tell me so many tales
of your adventures at sea…
I'm so glad you're friends with me.

Chapter Four

A Surfer and a Mermaid

Miranda swished her aqua tail. Water sprayed on Pablo.

"Hey," he said, shaking out his surfer locks. "Say, don't spray."

He plopped down on the craggy shore of the tiny island where he was marooned.

Pablo had been here since he crashed his surfboard several weeks before. At first it had been rough, but on the seventh day he had met Miranda.

She tossed her head. Her hair radiated out like a burst of electric snakes. Not exactly the sort of hair Pablo wanted to run his fingers through, yet there was something about her—when she smiled Pablo could see two rows of iridescent teeth lined up like tiny diamonds...or was it fish hooks?

Goosebumps prickled up and down his arms.

"What? Are you cold?" Miranda asked, enunciating every word as if she were speaking a foreign language. Without waiting for an answer she set down her whalebone needles and held up a shawl knit of seaweed. The smell of wet kelp filled the air.

He let her wrap him in the shawl. She pulled it tight around his neck.

"Don't hurt me," he said, grabbing her arm.

Her eyes flashed then narrowed. *Like snake eyes*, Pablo thought. But her next words were soft like a lullaby.

"Don't be cross," she cooed. "Let me feed you."

She shimmied into the shallow water. When she emerged, her arms were full of wriggling fish. Tuna, cichlids, puffer fish, angelfish, some clams and a stingray.

"Sushi surprise," she said. Her teeth glinted in the sun.

Pablo blanched, but he was hungry. He accepted a clam. He broke it open and scraped out the gooky center. It tasted salty and grainy, yet warm and comforting. It was both wonderful and terrible at the same time. Like Miranda.

He ate the rest of the fish Miranda skinned and scaled for him. She sang while he ate. In her silvery soprano she sang a song about all the fish in the great blue sea. After awhile Pablo began to feel the fish were not in the sea, but instead swimming in his middle. He could feel them flopping and flipping. His face and head grew hot.

She's put a spell on me, he thought.

He moaned as Miranda's song spiraled upward into a howl. It sounded like a siren whirling in his head.

His eyes twitched and crossed. His head nodded. He fell into a sleep as deep as the ocean from which he had been flung. He withered into a heap on the wet beach. He didn't see Miranda wiping his brow and scooting his feet away from the tide that lapped at them.

However, once during the feverish night he awoke immersed in a dream of a large fish with teeth sharp like a shark's. He screamed and batted at Miranda. She "oohed" and "ahhed" him back to sleep.

The next morning he gingerly opened one eye. His fever was gone. The only heat he felt was from the sun's rising rays, stretched like a witch's fingers scraping the sky. He opened his other eye. A bandicoot rat skittered by. A yellow-bellied weasel scampered after it. Miranda was not sitting next to him. He sat up. She was not on the beach at all. He stood up. He could not see her anywhere along the sea line.

Pablo paced the shore. He was cold. He was hungry. He was also something else he could not name.

"What have I done?" he asked the mynas, who only screeched back.

"Miranda," he wailed, wading into the tide. *Wait.* Was that her or a swooping seagull that flashed in and out of the waves?

"I must see," he said. He stripped bark off a rubber tree. He interlaced the bark with seaweed. He made a raft; small and round like a basket.

He filled it with passion fruit and mangoes to eat and loose leaves to sit upon, leaving a little space for himself in the middle. Gingerly he stepped into the raft. It gave with his weight, slopping in the waves, but it did not sink.

He raised the sail he shaped from the shawl Miranda made. He bobbled up and down on one wave and another. Soon his fruit ran out. The sun beat down. The leaves got soggy. He was a surfer, not a sailor. At first he cursed. Then he screamed, but finally he sang a song of loneliness and love lost. His song joined with the sad songs of the whales and dolphins. It was a sea symphony that expanded and grew so that the very waves seemed to keep time.

And in the midst of it all he heard a soprano voice. *Miranda?* He stood up to see, shifting his raft into a wave. The basket rose on the wave's crest and for a minute he was surfing! Then smash! Crash! He slammed the waters. Pieces of rubber and grass exploded about him as he flailed to keep his head above water. The waves rolled him along. He couldn't get free. He thrashed and he writhed but he could not break the surface. Down, down he sank into the depths. Like a fish drinking air he breathed in the sea.

He saw his life swim before his eyes until, all of a sudden he felt himself being lifted. Slowly, slowly he was tugged to shore.

He slept for three days and three nights. On the third day he opened his eyes. Miranda. She had him wrapped in seaweed blankets. The smell of rotten fish and dead kelp permeated the air. Miranda inhaled and moved toward him as if she were going to resuscitate him. Pablo pulled back until he noticed the tears on her face sparkling like diamonds. He let the kiss be.

"Welcome home," she said, her smile sitting like a half moon lying on its side. Her tail shone in the sunlight, brilliant and magnificent. For the first time, Pablo realized what having no legs might mean.

"Ahh, let *me* feed *you*," Pablo said. He walked into the jungle tangled like a tropical garden to look for the fruits she could not reach and the roots she had never tasted. When he looked back she was looking toward the tide washing up and then away. Pablo's heart leaped. Could it ever be—a mermaid and a surfer sharing the beach and the sea?

Soon his arms grew heavy with the load of coconuts and kiwis he had picked from the trees. He stumbled back to her and laid them at what on an ordinary woman would be her feet. She picked up a kiwi and bit into it. Juice squirted onto Pablo's cheek. He laughed and so did she.

""I have never tasted anything so sweet," she said. Pablo blushed, and the rest is history.

Chapter Five

Poems of the Heart

Best Friends

"I'm a feminista artiste,"
said the diva to the queen,
"I make new glories from the horrors I've seen.
I make and create.
I sing the divine.
I take heartbreak and heartsick
and make it sublime."
The queen was impressed, pressing her hand to her heart.
"I, myself am starting a new start.
I lead the fairies. I'm magic and smart.
I am a dreamer. I fly in the stars,
I bring back gold
for czarinas and czars.
I like to draw. I like to write."
"Oooh," said the diva,
"Let's dance in the light.
We are a good team or so it seems!"
So the diva became best friends with the queen
each helping the other to grow the best dreams.

Two-Act Play

A wicked rat wrapped in scraps
tried to get a part in a one act play
but he couldn't remember his lines—
He could only remember mine.
So…
the director, a former famous friend,
gave him my part because he liked
the way
the light glinted on the rat's saber sharp teeth.
I left the stage in tears.

I ran to my cold attic apartment
where I live with kind mice.
They cursed the rat with me—they are so sweet and nice.
I wrote them a play with two acts
(take that you stupid rat)
and now we, me and the mice, are all famous!
You may kiss our feat
but don't show your
teeth.
We're funny about that.

Wish

The cupboard sits silent—
the mice all gone.
The linoleum is nervous,
the sink basin calm.
The witch in the kitchen cackles no more.
I've nailed up the windows.
I wish for a door.

Chapter Six

Nella's Feminist Tale

Nella and Betsy
lived in the top of a house,
Betsy was a black widow spider, Nella—a mouse.
They both shared the attic of a feminist with flair...
Genevieve Lilliput Marcella St Claire.
It was 1946 France. Change was in the air.
The attic was full of trunks spilling over with stuff,
petticoats, corsets and used powder puffs.
The creaky floor was littered with quilts,
the walls were hung with exotic silks.
Important papers were mixed with trash.
There were garlands of lace and other fancy panache.
Holey Persian rugs snuffed out most of the drafts.
Nella had shredded an old dress for her bed.
Lying in it chatting with Betsy in her web,
this day they were discussing how sugar and spice
influence poverty leading to vice
as strands of conversation wound their way
up through the walls.
They could hear Genevieve talking
with her friend Jacque Pall.
Jacque Pall asked, "What is a man?"
Genevieve halted but then she began,
"Well, not a mouse nor any vermin,
but most of all not a woman."
"Ahh, that is as it should be," Jacque Pall said confidently.
"Except," Genevieve said, with her natural bold flair,

"Women, you notice, aren't treated fair.
We don't make the same money nor have the same rights.
It's a struggle for most of us just to survive."
And though she said more, her voice drifted off.
The ladies upstairs had heard enough. Nella stood up,
shocked and appalled.
Betsy almost fell off of the wall.
"Can you believe it?' Nella said, "She is just like us."
"Treated unfair?" Betsy responded, "Or making a fuss?"
"Either way, she's made my day. Didn't you hear what she
had to say?
We are females, hear freedom ring!"
Nella squeaked trying to sing
"Just a second," Betsy implored, choking demurely on a fly
wing,
"We are treated wrong, me and you. We are treated like
vermin;
this is true, not because we are women
but because we are not human."
"What!" Nella said jumping off of her bed.
"Whose side are you on? Are you out of your head?
Do you want to be a pawn and end up dead?"
"Oh, give it a rest, this isn't chess.
As spiders, mice, bats and rats
we are hardly thought of as aristocrats!
It doesn't matter if we're a girl or a boy—
as mice and spiders we are the hoi polloi."
Nella stared at her, clearly annoyed.
"Oh, dear," she said, and then had to stop.
Wiggling her whiskers she stalked off.
Betsy wrung her hands, all eight
then she stood up yelling,
"Wait! Wait! Wait!
I am right, but so are you.
We are oppressed, it is true,

both as vermin and as women.
If we are to make everything right
we've got to choose which battle to fight.
We'll no longer be pests.
We'll be our female best!"
The two girls set to work in frenzied fuss.
The very air was electric with all they discussed.
"We will write speeches," Nella said
Betsy added, "And make a flag."
"And have a rally and a parade!"
The pals worked all night, oh, the things they made.
Thoughts and ideas turned into songs
"Give us our rights.
Don't give us your wrongs.
We are not riffraff, trash or tramps
We aren't floozies, wantons or vamps.
Spiders and mice are mainly nice.
Don't make us turn our versas into vice!"
It didn't matter if they made sense
It only mattered that they incensed.
They ventured out of the attic and into the street
where they threw out crumbs, saying,
"Let us eat cake."
They preached to squirrels and sparrows, pigeons and bats,
to rats and mice and lice in hats.
Random moles and opossums wandering by
were lassoed in by their fervent cries.
Soon the city was alive
buzzing like bees drunk in a hive
They danced and whirled in an unsteady parade,
on this day in France when history was made.
Nella and Betsy marched ahead
as all of the others were more or less led
like lemmings to the cliff but none ended up dead,
nor did they plummet like a Thelma or Louise

but they sang and they shouted not pretty but pleased.
They sang,
"We are females, girls and ladies!
We're not demons from the depths of Hades
nor pesty vermin, full of rabies!"
Soon the female spiders, squirrels and rats
were joined by female ferrets and parrots,
dogs and cats.
Their singing rose, ringing through the air
into the sitting room of Genevieve Lilliput Marcella St Claire.
She and Jacque Pall walked out their front door,
dropping their hats to the well waxed floor.
"Oh, no, bless our souls! We better call pest control,"
both of them sighed turning together, returning inside.
But actually, Genevieve did no such thing.
She brightly recognized freedom's ring.
Using her pen as a sword to fight,
she went on to write about women's rights
and though no evidence will you find
she probably had Nella and Betsy on her mind.

Chapter Seven

Poems of Self

Sellfe E'Steem

Sellfe E'Steem is full of herself.
She feels pretty good.
You never hear Sellfe E'Steem
or
anyone else
go around saying,
"Sellfe E'Steem is stupid"
or
"Sellfe E'Steem is ugly"
or
"Sellfe E'Steem is too fat."
Even if Sellfe E'Steem is too fat,
it gets spelled
phat
and is a good thing.
That is Sellfe E'Steem's way.
You can't fault her for that.

Sadness Wears a Hat with a Feather on Top

Sadness came to visit me
on a day I didn't expect.
She let herself in a window
like a bird without respect.
I gave her tea, bread & chocolate cake.
She ate all night, keeping me awake
telling tales & crooning songs.
I couldn't get her to leave & to leave her would be wrong,
so I made her a room & gave her a phone.
Now she chats up my friends but leaves me alone.

Magic Mirror

A sad, forlorn fairy
hurt and betrayed…
She thought she was loved
when she was tricked by charade.
The word love seemed to float through the air
but when she tried to catch it was not there.
Whatever.
Some fairies just need to take a warm bath
and notice what they already have…
and if
not enough is near
they can always look harder
or buy a new mirror.

Chapter Eight

The Strange Her

Once there was a man and a woman who did not have a child.

"I wish we had a child," the man said.

"I wish I had a daughter," the woman said. Soon thereafter a young girl came knocking upon their door. Boy, were they surprised. They weren't sure at first if they should let her in but they *had* wished for a daughter. They let her in.

They thought she was an odd-looking child.

"She does not look like me," the woman said.

"She does not look like me," the man said.

"I look like myself," the girl said.

The man and woman didn't know what she meant by *that*, but they had prayed for a child.

She must be some part of God's will," the woman said, looking askance at her husband.

"Where shall we put her?" asked the man.

"Where will she go?" asked the woman.

"I am **here**," said the girl.

"We will place you in the center," the woman said

They made a room for her in the middle of their house. They painted the room with faith. They furnished it with hope. Any worry they might have had they stuffed in the closet.

69

For a while, things went very well. The girl stayed in her room. The man and woman worked feverishly to make everything right for her. The woman vacuumed the house. The man took out the trash. They spent money on her for everything they thought she might need. They were sincere and careful shoppers

"Only the best food," the woman said.

"Only the best clothes," the man said.

"I would like some hip-hop CDs," the girl said

"What?" the woman said, flapping her hand about her head as if she were chasing away gnats.

And that is when things started changing. The woman soon noticed the house had a different odor. It no longer smelled like an overcast sunrise but more like January dusk with a taste of snow in the air.

She discovered doors that should be opening *out* were opening *in*. When she went down into the basement to do laundry she found herself up in the attic. When she later went to the attic to retrieve an old lamp she found herself in the basement.

"Oh, my!" she cried. "I must sit down." She plopped down where her favorite chair usually was and almost broke her bottom. All the furniture was on the ceiling!

"Maybe I am hypoglycemic and just need to eat," she said out loud, fanning herself. She went in the kitchen to make a grilled cheese. She opened the refrigerator door and was shocked by the blast of warm air that came out. All the eggs inside were fried and the milk was boiling frothily. She slammed the door in a fit of snit. She opened the oven to remove the frying pan she kept there and was surprised by the cool air wafting out.

"It is *that* girl! She is causing all these changes. We'll just see about this," the woman exclaimed, dialing 911.

"Hello, hello," she shouted into the phone. The only answer back was static. The woman wasn't sure if it was the police dispatcher or if it was *that girl*. The woman sputtered when she meant to mutter. She cried when she meant to sigh. She said, "never mind" instead of "hold the line." She hung up when she meant to speak up.

She snagged her husband as he hurried by.

"Things are not right," she said, pulling on his belt as if she was reeling in a fish.

"I don't know what you are talking about," he said, unhooking her fingers from his belt.

"Can't you see?" she asked. "The furniture is on the ceiling! I can't very well sit on the couch and use the chandelier for a coffee table. The coffee keeps spilling."

"Hmm," the man said, "I should think having the furniture on the ceiling would make dusting easier."

Neither saw the girl watching from the bedroom.

"How about the doors!" the woman went on, her eyes batting so fast it looked like they might fly right out of her head. "I go *into* a room and find I am coming *out*."

The man raised his eyebrows, sauntered over to the closet and pulled the door open.

"I believe it has always opened this way," he said.

"Well, then the attic and the basement. How about them? They have traded places!" The woman was definitely screeching now.

"My dear," the man said patiently, "I think it might turn out quite useful to have the basement in the attic when it comes time to repair the sump pump. And with the attic in the basement I think we may have less trouble with bats, hmm?"

The woman crossed her eyes. The girl shut her door quietly, though some might have thought it opened.

"I have work to do," the man said. He left.

"Okay, it is up to me. I will get to 'the bottom of this or the top of it or the middle of it or, oh, dear!" the woman cried. She strung garlic around her neck and put a charm bracelet around her wrist. She put on her makeup heavier than usual so that it almost looked like war paint. She looked toward the girl's room. She didn't trust someone as strange as her.

She waited until evening then tiptoed to the girl's room. She placed her ear inconspicuously against the door. She heard music, strange music. The melody jangled where one would expect it to jingle. It was dominated by sharps when flats would have been so much more harmonic. The woman heard the girl crooning lyrics that made no sense to her. The woman tried to hum along, but she could not match the tune. The sounds that came from her sounded like bellowing.

The girl opened the door.

"Yes?" she said expectantly.

The woman stood with her mouth opening and closing so that she looked not unlike a goldfish.

The girl narrowed her eyes. Her lips tightened.

The woman stepped back as if she had been seared with a laser. Her face reddened and puffed out.

The girl's cheeks sank in and her nostrils flared.

Then suddenly the woman turned on her heel and stomped off just as the girl slammed her door. The "Enter at Your Own Risk" sign flapped against the door.

Cold tears fell from the woman's eyes. She wrapped herself in a cloak. She walked into the living room, tripping over the slowly whirring ceiling fan attached now to the floor. She felt anger ripple through her body like a newly discovered muscle. She flexed it. She felt filled with energy.

"I will not be a victim," she cried out, as if someone were listening.

She took a deep breath, exhaling slowly and completely. It was as if a southerly wind breezed through the room. The woman grabbed a broom and beat the rugs. Some of her anger wafted out with the dust. She then laid the rugs on the ceiling so the furniture could properly rest upon them. She whipped all the perishables into the oven to keep them cool. She shivered, chilling out as a little more anger fell away. She dusted all those places it had been hard to reach before. The stretching knocked off the last few flecks of anger. The house glittered like gold.

"I love everything sparkling," she said, as she danced through the house.

The girl peeked from out of her room. The woman didn't panic. The girl slipped one foot out, pointing it out as if she were a ballerina. The woman busied herself watering artificial flowers. The girl slipped her other foot out and the rest of her body followed.

The woman thought she heard birds singing a cheery song of summer.

The girl thought she heard bats bleating a dirge of doom. Her eyes narrowed. Her lips tightened.

The woman set down her broom and faced the girl.

The girl couldn't tell if it was the room sparkling or the woman's eyes.

"Hello," the woman said softly.

"Hello," the girl said, her voice on the edge, wanting to brighten.

"Are you hungry for dinner?' the woman asked.

For a moment there was only the sound of the two of them breathing.

Then the girl answered. "No, I am Gretel."

The woman's eyes grew very wide, but then she relaxed. She laughed. The girl laughed with her.

"Glad to meet you," the woman said smiling. "You can call me Mother."

She held out her hand and Gretel took it. They walked into the kitchen. Gretel snapped open the blinds and sunshine flooded the room. The mother pulled a saucepan from the china cabinet. Gretel snatched plates out of the silverware drawer. Together they cooked a delicious dinner and set the table for three. The father came home minutes later. Together they ate a family dinner.

Afterwards the father said, "I feel like dessert."

"I feel like dessert," the mother said. "How about you, Gretel? What do you feel like?"

"I feel like a daughter," Gretel said, as she watched a sprinkling of sugar waft down to the ceiling where they were seated.

"Or, maybe..." she continued, "just maybe pineapple upside down cake would hit the spot."

They all laughed as more sugar fell like snow on a summer evening.

Chapter Nine

Poems of Belief

Lucky You

You are so wonderful to have such luck.
I wonder if you'll let me have just a little to wear
around my neck?
Come sit next to me and tell me how your garden grows
and what you do with the spiders,
the mice and the sparrows.
In the winter what you do with the snow?
You make angels, I bet,
that you then photograph and send
to aborigines
who are afraid to do it for themselves.
God smiles funny when He sees me
but I think He laughs when He sees you.
Come sit next to me and
tell me what to do so I can be lucky, too…
I will do as you say as long as it plays out as play
I am so happy to have such luck as you.

Renaissance

If life were magic this is how it would be:
What I wanted would come true
but mostly I would know what it is I wanted.
Good things would come to me without me even asking.
When I did ask, no one would get mad even if they had to
say, "No."
There would be synchronicity.
My dreams would have meaning.
I would be able to have some supernatural abilities or in other
ways feel divine.
I would be able to draw people and things to me.
I would lead a charmed and blessed life.
I would have intimate knowledge and/or communication with
angels, ghosts or saints.
I would see the magic in everyday life.
I would be able to participate in small miracles.
I would see large miracles all around me.
I would be blessed with true talent that resulted in art that
others would see and appreciate, leading me to great success.
I would be loved and respected.
I would be fully me.

Monkey Princess

"Love yourself fierce, living life free,"
a monkey princess said to me.
"No matter what gnomes of doubt
surround you with their hateful shouts,
shrug them off like grizzly bears eating taffy at a fair
and fill yourself with wild-felt glee,
sugar water, love and me…
because, my dear, there's nothing else but living life loving
self.
Every girl should be a queen and every boy a someday king.
Fly, my love, with lovely wings
across the world to see its best,
stopping often to love the rest."
I follow now what she said to me,
loving life loving me.

Chapter Ten

Dragon of Never More

It was a hot July night,
the heat like a blanket, thick and quilted
I sweated all over, my hair limp and wilted.
I hid in the sycamores,
my horse in the willows.
I felt my breath on my hand
like tears on a pillow.
I waited for the Dragon of Never More.
I waited like the rich wait for the poor
to hold out their hands
cracked and sore.
I would fight to the death no matter the gore.
I waited all night into the noon;
waited like soup waits for a spoon…
when there came
A crack! A crash! A whoosh! A whoop!
I spit spit as if it were the soup.
The dragon flew in like the dead heading east
chomping her fangs for her poisoned feast.
I drew my blade and cut my thumb
I did not cry
I was too numb.
I flashed my sword into the sky
screaming at the dragon, "Die! Die! Die!"
She flapped her wings
and sparked her teeth.
She kicked her legs and flexed her feet.

I jumped upon her arching back
wrestling her mane
which like snakes attacked.
I cut off her hair, her nose, her ears!
She scorched my eyebrows, my cheeks, my fears.
The fight was fearsome. It went on for days
but she slowly calmed down as I learned her ways.
Now we are friends as if we care.
She licks my wounds, I curl her hair.
People may say,
"What an odd pair!"
They don't know hate is
love not treated fair.
We right the wrong in nursery songs
making a place where we belong.
This is our myth's only hope—
to be more together
than alone can cope.

Chapter Eleven

Poems of the Soul

Lost in the Woods

A home in the woods
where it's leafy and dark…
spiders and termites and scraps of bark…
smelling of rot and loggy decay.
But a home is a home, come what may.
And what does come
tumbling through the twiggy limbs
of the stretchy trees,
like a nightmare rolling
on a stormy breeze?
I close the door of sticks and brass
knowing safety will not last.
The wind grows large. It whips my home
into piggy pieces as if a wolf's just blown.
I run through the forest praying to hide
bearing false hope like one bares pride.
But there's nowhere to go when there's not a home,
there's nowhere to go to be alone.

Star

I felt like a Star in the deepest night,
hope inciting a special place
now shining in the light…
but was it not just the moon reflecting back
what is really mine?
I must keep the Star somewhere in my mind
so poetry and art can kiss the divine.
Can I do it alone…
recreating my own light from that shine once shown?
As surely as my life proceeds
I walk with a torch to
light my needs.
Yes, I am a Star,
to those who can see.
I am a Star if I want to be.

Faith

I am a diva with wings.
I am a poet with strength.
I am a love
that knows not her fate yet
but I grow in beauty, my secrets kept…
knowing truth will kiss away my sweat
when the time has come and God shines green,
when the future breaks
like an emerald gleams.
In faith I create,
live and wait.
God loves me like I trust fate.

Chapter Twelve

Meeting Psyche

Part I

"I like water but I am not a water nymph," Lucy said to no one in particular. She looked down into the pond at her reflection to make sure. Her reflection glimmered in the still water. Lucy sighed and slipped her toes into the water, right into the reflection of her nose. Ripples spread out making Lucy giggle.

It was not much fun to giggle alone. But what choice did she have? Lucy had never had a real friend. She wondered what a friend would be like. *It might be scary. How about if the friend doesn't like me? How about if the friend thinks I am weird? How about if they laugh at me? Am I smart enough to have friends? Am I okay enough to have a friend?*

She watched the gold fish skim through the water, making little waves.

"Fish I may, fish I might, have the fish I fish tonight." Lucy said. She stuck her forefinger into the water hoping a fish might come up and lick it or do whatever it is fish do when they make your acquaintance. The fish swam under a frog floating by on top of a big broad leaf.

"Hello, Frog," she said.

The frog croaked and fell off the leaf, splashing into the water. *What the…*

"I must look ghastly," she said looking back into the pond for her reflection. This time she saw another face next to hers reflected back. She gasped; the other face was so beautiful. She looked up and to her right to see a small man or large boy smiling at her. His smile sparkled like the water.

"Hello," he said, "I am Narcissus. Can I sit with you?"

He flopped his hair into his eyes. Lucy could not tell whether he was squinting or winking.

"I know I barely know you, but I already feel close to you and feel like I can tell you anything," Narcissus said. He batted his seaweed green eyes at her as he reached for her hand. Lucy's hand was wet and clammy. His felt warm and strong.

"I've been feeling pretty low," he continued, sighing. "Sometimes when I look in the lake I see this serpent. I really, really do. At least I think I do. No, I believe I do. Anyway, it's green and hideous. I look away. I like looking at you. Are you a serpent?"

"Oh, me? No," Lucy blushed, shocked and unsure. "But I've seen demons in the woods in the deepest dark among the giant trees. I know what you mean."

"Oh, yes, yes, yes! You do, too. I can tell!" Narcissus said, looking intently into Lucy's eyes that were quite blue, like a clear lake on a sunny day.

Narcissus kept his eyes locked on Lucy's. She felt as if he were searching for something…something. After a while Lucy began to feel like her breath was his. She could almost feel her heart pounding in his chest. It was a different sort of feeling. She wondered if this is what it felt like to be in love.

Suddenly Narcissus cried out, "Let's play!" He did not break eye contact as he leapt up into the dive position.

"Okay," Lucy agreed quickly. She jumped into the pool. By herself.

Narcissus balanced his bronzed, muscled body on the edge of the bank. A look of deep concern crossed his face like a cloud drifting in front of the sun.

"Are you okay?" he asked.

Lucy answered by flipping into a fancy dive, then paddling to the shallow water.

"Yes."

"Well, maybe I can just get my feet a little wet," Narcissus said as he plopped down on the side of the lake.

He dangled his foot in the water, giggling. Lucy liked the sound of his giggle in the same way she liked the sound of soda pop glooping, glipping out of a long necked bottle. She wondered what his full-throated laughter sounded like.

"Let's play," she said. She yanked his foot. She laughed as his golden body lost balance and SPLASH! He was in the water with her.

But, somehow, oh, no! The water suddenly seemed deeper and Narcissus was not laughing. He was choking...or was he drowning? Lucy threw her arms around his neck, thrashing to keep their heads above water. Narcissus clung tight, at first, but then he began flailing his arms.

"We're heading into deeper water—the serpents! You're taking me to the serpents. You have misled me. You are confusing me! Why are we swimming in our reflections?" he screamed, taking in a large gulp of pond water. He choked.

Lucy lost control. All would've probably come to some ghastly end if she hadn't let go when her own face turned blue. She sank, deep. *The water had been shallow, it had, it had, it had.* But now she sank, holding her breath with lips so tight she thought she would pass out. She sank. Far, far away she could hear Narcissus calling out to her...

"Save me, save me, I'm dying," is what it sounded like but then he might've been saying, "leave me, leave me, I'm crying."

Lucy didn't stay sunk for days or weeks or anything as improbable as that, but she did stay sunk for longer than she would've preferred and longer than she could hold her breath for. And too long for Narcissus to wait for her. When she came sputtering out, he was water skiing with some floozy he kept referring to as Echo. Try as she might, Lucy could not catch his attention.

Part II

Lucy was sitting around her cottage, situated quaintly, as cottages generally are, on the edge of an especially pretty forest. She was busy thinking. Thinking was her favorite thing to do, that and daydreaming or talking to a Tree she had met in the woods.

When Lucy first discovered the woods it was in spite of her own best efforts. She had been exhausted after the Narcissus fiasco, not to mention ill from gulping in all that rancid lake water. She spent agonizing months analyzing what she had done to make Narcissus go away. However, it slowly dawned on her that the problem was little more than the fact that Narcissus couldn't swim. Upon realizing this Lucy began skipping in a slow and methodical way and almost tripped over a little, tiny Tree struggling bravely in the midst of strangling vines and fungi-like mold. She set about untangling the vines and washing away the mold with her own spit and tears. Slowly, the little sapling began swaying and singing a precious sort of tree song. Lucy stopped her doting on it for a minute. She sat back to listen and noticed she was on the edge of the forest.

"Well, can you beat that?" she asked Tree.

"No, I don't believe in beating," Tree answered, "though I do have limbs so I guess I could if I wanted to, but I don't want to. How do *you* do?" he asked, reaching out a branch to her.

Lucy fell over.

"Ooops, sorry, I thought you wanted to be friends," Tree said.

"No, no, no," Lucy said, getting up and brushing herself off. "I mean, yes, yes, yes. I do want to be friends. No, you did not knock me down. I knocked my own self down."

"Wow, I don't think I can knock myself down with these roots and all. Is it fun?" Tree asked.

"Oh, Tree," Lucy said hugging him.

That was when she decided she would stay and she built a cottage. That was a long, long time ago. Lucy wasn't sure how long ago. She didn't keep time. She had tried, but it kept escaping her so finally, she had just let it go. Tree was now very large. When she leaned against him she felt warm and secure. He was kind and gentle. He never went away. He only laughed if he or she told a joke. The trouble was he had no eyes or hands or a mouth, for that matter, though she was able somehow to talk with him. And he was very smart as if he had soaked up ancient knowledge through roots that just kept growing and growing.

"You are such a good friend," she was saying when she noticed a shadow fall upon her. She turned quickly to see a half boy, half horse trot up to her and Tree.

"Hullo," he said with an affected English accent, "I am Petyr the Satyr."

He said this as it would mean something to her. *But how could that be?* Lucy thought. *I have never met him. I can hardly be held responsible for knowing people I don't know.* She reached out her hand in greeting.

Petyr kicked a stone.

"Sorry," he said, "I can't give you a hand. I need them both." He began laughing uproariously. Lucy just blushed.

"Uhm, do you know the way to the fairy ring?" he asked, composing himself as well as he could.

"Fairies? I have never seen any fairies around here."

Her heart skipped a beat as she thought how fun it might be to play with fairies. They would have wings to fly with. They would have legs to dance on.

"Well, I am suddenly not surprised," Petyr said, glancing around. "This does not seem to be a very socially active place."

Lucy felt like she was getting smaller and smaller. She looked at Tree who just waved his leaf-covered limbs in the wind as if he were some advertisement for Zen meditation. Lucy tried to hide behind him but, though he was a tall tree, he was not a broad tree.

"Well, we may not be active, but we are social," Lucy said, hoping that by talking tall she would not feel so small.

"I am so sorry if you feel slighted," Petyr said in a not very sorry way, "because I suppose you cannot help living in the sticks. But the issue is, is that I am on my way to only the coolest social event of the season. Queen Mab's coronation. Imagine that!"

"Queen who?" Lucy asked. She lived almost entirely in her imagination, but a Queen Mab had never been even a minor character in it.

"Really now, your ignorance is almost too much to bear. Queen Mab is the queen of the fairies," Petyr answered.

Lucy felt her face grow hot. The heat poured down into her body and, as if a match were lit, she blazed out,

"Well, pardon my ignorance, but if she is queen of the fairies, then obviously she is already a queen, so what does she need a coronation for?" Lucy fanned her sweating face.

"Listen once and listen well, because only once will I tell,' Petyr said as if he were casting a spell.

Lucy's eyes grew wide and dark like a black hole on a starless night. She let Petyr's words fall deep into her mind.

"She's been queen of the fairies, but now she's going to be queen of the Homo sapiens. The greatest honor of all," he whispered.

"Oh."

"Dyerwanna go?"

"Oh, no, not really, couldn't leave my Tree, you know."

"Your loss," Petyr whinnied, as he swished his tail and cantered away.

"Homo sapiens?" she asked, blinking and shaking her head.

"They're like you," Tree answered.

"Blue eyes? Blond hair? Whaddya mean?"

"Like you."

No one was like her. Fish were not like her. Frogs were not like her. She knew no one who talked to a tree or read her own poetry to the moon. Was Narcissus like her? Pretty. Intense. Knew of demons?

"Like me?"

Slowly Lucy felt like she was waking up from a dream. She cast a furtive glance around the forest. It *was* getting a bit overbearing, what with its great limbs stretching all about, dropping nuts on her head in a most annoying way. It was full of sticks and ticks. Her cottage was warm and safe, but it only held a tiny bed, one chair, one set of dishes.

But...

"Tree," she sought counsel again from her best friend, "would you go to Queen Mab's coronation?"

"Yeah, sure, just uproot myself and twaddle on over to see her, that's my plan," he answered.

"Um, no, I mean if you had legs, would you?"

"I don't."

"But, if you did?"

"Listen, Lucy, you do have legs. Do you want to go the coronation?"

"Oh, I couldn't leave you!"

"Oh, yeah, that's right. Who would I shade if not you?"

"So are you saying I should go?"

"I say follow your heart, to thine own self be true, march to the rhythm of your own drummer, ask not what your soul can do for you but what you..."

"Tree," Lucy interrupted, "I am happy here with you."

"Yes, and I love you, too, but that's not what you asked."

Lucy took a deep breath. The deeper it went into her middle, the taller she felt.

She touched Tree tenderly.

"I love you. I am leaving," she said.

"Yes, I understand. It was just a matter of time," Tree answered, weeping in his sappy way so that Lucy felt obliged to undo her knapsack and wipe away a bit of the sticky syrup so she could hug him.

"A girl's gotta do what a girl's gotta do," Tree said, as a way of goodbye.

Lucy smiled weakly as she stepped away from the edge of the forest. The sun seemed to shine a little too bright on the prairie grasses that stretched as far as she could see. Lucy froze. Her cottage, her Tree, her lovely forest were a little scary sometimes, but familiar. Who was Queen Mab? What were Homo sapiens and would she like them? How would she ever find them without even Petyr to follow? She looked at Tree who was waving a branch and singing.

"So long, goodbye, a happy farewell to you! Be good, be strong, and remember me in all you do..."

Lucy started crying so hard she had gone a hundred feet or so before she realized she had, indeed, started yet another journey.

Part III

It wasn't until the sixth night away from the forest that Lucy began to doubt her journey. It was an especially dark night. It seemed to get darker and darker toward morning, when, if Lucy remembered right, it should be getting lighter and lighter. Lucy shivered. It was very cold, an odd cold that seemed to have substance. The night air felt heavy upon her. Lucy felt her heart from the outside in, which was a very disturbing way to feel it.

She wrapped her jacket tightly about her. She trudged through the foggy blackness, gathering what twigs and dry grass she could forage. It was tedious work, but it gave her something to do to keep her mind from being swallowed by the dark. She was able to build quite a pile of debris yet when it came to light it...why, she had no matches!

I never have had matches, have I? Lucy wondered. Her head began feeling like it might spin away. *Then how did I light fires the other nights? Have I lit fires? If I haven't, then what's been keeping the night away? How have I stayed warm? I can't remember and I can't remember why I can't remember and, and, and...oh, it all seems so strange suddenly. Who am I? Where am I going? Why?*

She felt like the dark air joined in on the doubting questions, chilling her even further with its recriminations. Lucy cried out to confront the evil, but there was nothing to confront. There was only air. Heavy, dark, menacing air. Lucy tried to punch it. There was nothing to hit. She tried calling to Tree, but Tree was far away and had no legs, after all. The air was becoming heavier and Lucy could feel it breathing on her neck, her cheek...*No, No, No!* Then, for some odd reason, it seemed like it might be easier if she just gave in, just let the air take her, fill her. She could feel a tug of recognition deep in her nether regions, *yessss*, let the darkness touch her, kiss her, envelop her in its foul stench. *NOOOOOOOOO!*

No. She closed her eyes tight but tears somehow still spilled out. As powerfully and fully as young Lucy could, she called out, "HELP!"

She had no idea who could possibly help her, if anyone. She had never asked for help before. Yet that call bounded through the darkness. It flew as if it were a bird of deliverance, a nightingale, transforming her fervent plea into a beautiful song so that the moon came out to meet this One who could sing so wondrously true. Lucy lay by the unlit fire. She closed her eyes. *Oh, to sleep, perchance to dream...*

She didn't notice the silver sliver of moonlight touch upon a twig of Tree that was, curiously enough, clutched in her hand. SPARK! FLASH! Lucy opened her eyes in response to a glow of heat.

"YES!"

She lit the pile of broken branches and made a fire. It was a small fire and yet, so brilliant, a band of gypsies saw it from many miles away. Lucy did not know this, but she did know, somehow, that her journey was getting better. She kept the fire going, gathered a dinner of fruit and berries and grilled them over the fire. She was able to make a pie without the crust. It was not her favorite, but it was delicious in its own way.

She must have slept because the next day she awoke to the sun shining gloriously, welcoming her to the day with a hug of warmth. Lucy shaded her eyes, wondering if she was seeing things. A band of raggle-tag women wrapped in satin and velvet, loops of gold braid and silver netting fastened here and there to their billowing skirts walked her way. Their clothes were bright and gaudy in oranges and purples, yellows and greens. Their hair was unkempt and unruly with all the strands sticking out and about like rays from the sun. They had strung teeny, tiny bells about their ankles, their wrists and why, even in their glorious hair! They made sparkly, twinkly sounds as they walked.

As they came closer Lucy could see their eyes smiling. It made Lucy think they were saying 'hello, friend' in a language Lucy only knew in the depths of a memory she didn't remember having. The brightest of the gypsies stepped forward and offered her hand, turning it palm up and cupping it as if she was offering Lucy water. Lucy looked closer, but there was no water. *Or was there?* There did seem to be some sort of sparkling reflection. As Lucy reached out to touch the gypsy's hand the gypsy closed her fingers around Lucy's. Lucy thought she might feel some sort of exciting electrical charge or flurry of energy but she felt only fingers, warm fingers.

"Hello," the gypsy said. It sounded almost like she was singing.

"Hello," Lucy answered as she looked at the gentle faces surrounding her.

After last night's surprise success at staving off terror Lucy felt invincible, in a soft and vulnerable way. She felt safe enough to keep on talking.

"I am Lucy and I am going to see Queen Mab, queen of the fairies." Then, to her utter disbelief Lucy heard her voice continuing, "Do you want to come with me?"

Really, really, really she only asked because she believed their company might be delightful and not because she hoped against hope they'd be able to protect her from the Night. *Be good, be strong* she remembered as if from a long ago dream. Lucy quickly shook her head, moving her hand up to her face as if she were trying to brush a wisp of hair from her eyes.

The gypsies didn't even blink, but the one whom Lucy later came to know as Mary did answer, "Sure. Who is Queen Mab?"

Lucy was taken by surprise. So she wasn't the only one who hadn't known.

"I don't know," Lucy heard herself answer before she could censor her reply to make it cool and off hand. Now she felt really stupid. She braced herself to face the onslaught of the gypsies' laughter. They did not laugh. They didn't say, 'How do you know Queen Mab even exists' or 'We don't believe in fairies.'

They did say, "Hmm, you are like us."

Lucy felt a warm glow inside of her as if Tree's moonlit fire was inside of her own solar plexus.

She said in wonder, "I am?"

"Yes, you know of Faith."

"Faith? No, I don't believe I've made her acquaintance." Then they all did laugh, but it was a nice sort of laugh that made Lucy's fire glow a little warmer.

Later on, after they had breakfasted and were walking along all cozy in their soft moccasins, tiny bells tinkling and wafts of frankincense and frangipani sifting between them, Lucy risked again.

"I know you are gypsies and all, but are you also, by any remote chance, Homo sapiens?"

Mary looked at the gypsy next to her whose hair was red and curly, almost reaching her knees. It shined like it was sprinkled with stars.

"I do believe we are Homo sapiens, are we not?"

"Yes," her cohort answered, "that is our formal name, but I prefer to use the term human."

"So what shall I call you?" Lucy asked in a voice that was gentle and soft as if she were whispering in a church or a temple.

" Psyche," she said, tilting her head in such a way that the light of her eyes seemed to flutter and float about. Lucy felt very light herself. She also felt her heart beating from the inside out in that rhythmic, comforting way she remembered from so long ago. Lucy had at long last come home, which was odd because she had never had a home quite like she found among the gypsy-type humans who spoke so readily and freely of their friends, Faith and Innocence.

Epilogue

They never did see Queen Mab's coronation, but they did watch the sun rise over the mountains every morning, crowning their horizon so that their adventures were well lit and generally more playful than not. Lucy planted the twig that had fostered her fire that alarming night so long ago. She and the gypsies helped it to grow and nurtured it to fruition. They then packed the fruit to eat as they went about singing to the moon and lovingly strewing about the seeds so that more and more trees grew. They often talked with these trees when they weren't talking with one another.

At night the air still became heavy at times, but they found that if they huddled together and laughed, saying it wasn't the heat but the humidity, that the menacing forces would scuttle away like startled beetles into the depths of the shadows and they could fall asleep to dream their own joyous dreams.